USBORNE FIRST READING
Level Three

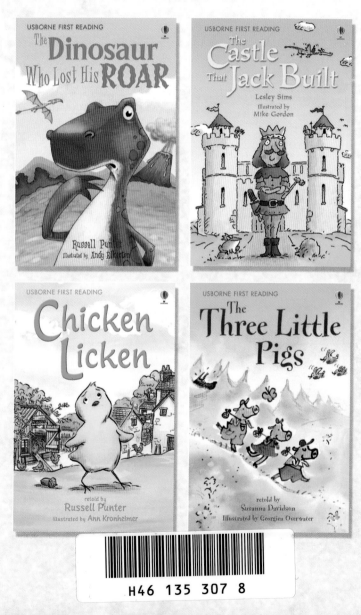

Chicken Licken

Retold by Russell Punter

Illustrated by

Ann Kronheimer

Reading Consultant: Alison Kelly
Roehampton University

This is a story about

Chicken
Licken

Henny
Penny

Cocky
Locky

Ducky
Lucky

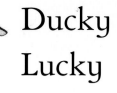

Goosey
Loosey

Turkey
Lurkey

and
Foxy Loxy.

This is where they live.

woods

farmyard

duck pond

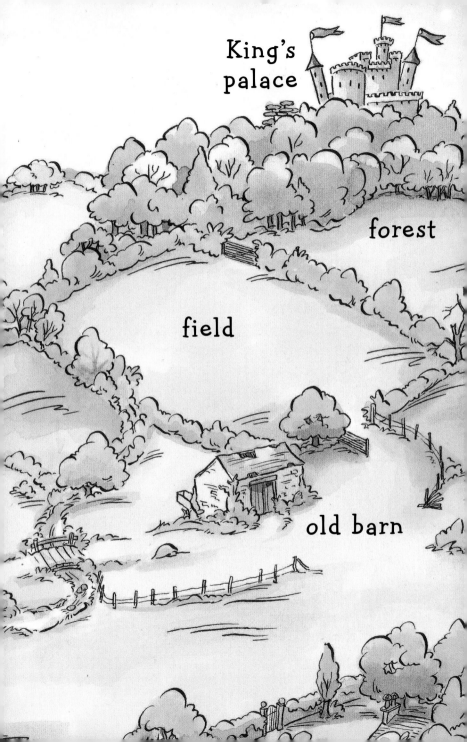

Once upon a time, there was a farm.

Most of the animals on
the farm were happy.

But Chicken Licken
wasn't happy.

Chicken Licken was scared – of everything.

One day, Chicken Licken
went to the woods.

He stopped by an
oak tree.

Suddenly, a tiny acorn
dropped from the tree

and hit Chicken Licken's head.

Chicken Licken didn't see the acorn.

He looked up at the
blue sky.

"Oh no!" he said. "The
sky must be falling."

Chicken Licken ran
around the tree.

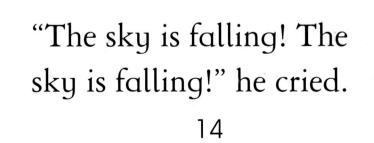

"The sky is falling! The
sky is falling!" he cried.

"I must tell the King," thought Chicken Licken.

He rushed back to the farmyard.

Henny Penny was sitting by the hen house.

"Out of my way!" yelled Chicken Licken.

"What's the matter?"
asked Henny Penny.

"The sky is falling!" cried
Chicken Licken.

17

"Oh no!" said Henny
Penny. "What shall
we do?"

"I'm going to warn the
King," said Chicken
Licken.

"I'll come too," said
Henny Penny.

They ran past the hen
house and... **Thump!**

They bumped into
Cocky Locky.

"What's the matter?"
asked Cocky Locky.

"The sky is falling!" cried
Chicken Licken.

"Oh no!" said Cocky
Locky. "What shall
we do?"

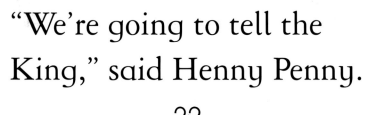

"We're going to tell the
King," said Henny Penny.

22

"I'll come too," said
Cocky Locky.

They ran out of the
farmyard.

They ran past the
duck pond.

Ducky Lucky was
swimming.

"What's the matter?"
he asked.

"The sky is falling!" cried
Chicken Licken.

"Oh no!" said Ducky
Lucky. "What shall
we do?"

"We're going to tell the
King," said Cocky Locky.

"I'll come too," said
Ducky Lucky.

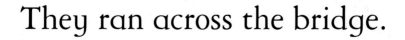

They ran across the bridge.

They came to the old barn.
Goosey Loosey was sitting
on her nest.

"What's the matter?" she
asked.

"The sky is falling!" cried
Chicken Licken.

"Oh no!" said Goosey
Loosey. "What shall
we do?"

"We're going to tell the
King," said Ducky Lucky.

"I'll come too," said
Goosey Loosey.

They ran past the barn.

They ran into the field.

Turkey Lurkey was
pecking at the ground.

32

"What's the matter?" she asked.

"The sky is falling!" cried Chicken Licken.

"Oh no!" said Turkey Lurkey. "What shall we do?"

"We're going to tell the King," said Goosey Loosey.

34

"I'll come with you," said
Turkey Lurkey.

They ran through the field.

Soon, they came to the forest – and Foxy Loxy.

"What's the matter?" he asked.

"The sky is falling!" cried Chicken Licken.

Foxy Loxy didn't think the sky was falling. But he didn't say.

"We're going to tell the King," said Turkey Lurkey.

"I know a shortcut," said Foxy Loxy.

He led them into the
forest...

and pointed to a hole.
"Down here," he said.

They all went down
the hole.

"Is this where the King
lives?" asked Henny Penny.

"No," said Foxy Loxy.
"It's where I live."

"And it's where I'm going
to gobble you all up!"

"Who will tell the King the sky is falling?" cried Chicken Licken.

"Stupid bird," said Foxy Loxy. "The sky can't fall."

42

Just then, an acorn hit
Foxy Loxy on the head.

Foxy Loxy didn't see it.

All he could see was sky.

Now he was scared.

He ran down the tunnel
and was never seen again.

The others had seen the
acorn fall on Foxy Loxy.

Everyone looked at
Chicken Licken.

"Are you sure the sky fell
on your head?" they said.

"Maybe it was an acorn,"
said Chicken Licken.

And they chased him all
the way home.

Chicken Licken is a very old folk tale. No one knows who first wrote it, but it may come from a similar story in the *Jataka* – a collection of Buddhist tales. That version of the story features a rabbit instead of a chicken.

Series editor: Lesley Sims

First published in 2007 by Usborne Publishing Ltd., Usborne House, 83-85 Saffron Hill, London EC1N 8RT, England. www.usborne.com
Copyright © 2007 Usborne Publishing Ltd.

USBORNE FIRST READING
Level Four